WHISPERS OF THE INVISIBLES

NACHIKETA AND THE MYSTERY OF THE DARK SHADOWS

WHISPERS OF THE INVISIBLES- NACHIKETA AND THE MYSTERY OF THE DARK SHADOWS

ISBN –978-93-5268-253-9

Published by-
Badal Paul
Kashibati, Raiganj, Uttar Dinajpur
West Bengal -733134
Mob- 91-9434961092
Email-getbadalpaul@gmail.com

Publisher-Badal Paul
First Published in 2017
Published From- Raiganj, Uttar Dinajpur,
West Bengal-733134

Typeset and Printing by Coral Printing Press,

Raiganj, Uttar Dinajpur, West Bengal.

About The Author

Badal Paul is an educator, blogger, and writer. A bookworm, Badal Paul keeps immense interest in Kriya Yoga, ancient history, occult knowledge, paranormal activities and parapsychology. The author keeps a keen interest in writing poems, novels and short stories. "WHISPERS OF THE INVISIBLES" is an unmatched paranormal detective story series which comes with the first book under the title of "NACHIKETA AND THE MYSTERY OF THE DARK SHADOWS". Besides, the author has penned another novel - "KALCHAKRA –OOM AND THE CHOSEN FIVE". It is his debutant novel by Roman Books. The author is working in the next six parts of the same series. Born in 1982, the author had a struggling life and presently lives at Raiganj, West Bengal, India with his loved wife and mother.

License Notes

ACKNOWLEDGEMENT

I am indebted to umpteen number of people for inspiring me to make the book reality for the readers, which is undoubtedly going to delight and amuse the readers to the very core of their spirit.

My family had been my constant support in the nocturnal hours when I was digging deep inside the making of the book.

I can not deny the love and support I got from my friends, relatives, students, patrons and the readers of my books.

The highest gratitude goes to the man behind the name NACHIKETA and the sages who have in multiferous ways inspired me to create this book.

Lastly, the people who consider me at the bitter end are my utmost inspiration.

Thanks.

Contents

Introduction

Dr Sen, a famous doctor in *Kalimpong*, a hill station, buys a house named *The Seventh Heaven*. He is disturbed because of his daughter's sudden but strange change of behaviour. He meets with *Manab*, a patient who warns him about his garden which is mysterious. *Dr Sen* ignores the words of *Manab* considering him an insane. At a friendly get-together, *Dr Sen* comes to know about the personal experience of *Dr.Chatterjee* and about the unbelievable abilities of *Dr Nachiketa*. *Dr Chatterjee* acquaints all how his son *Soham* mysteriously fell ill and how while travelling on the train they met *Dr Nachiketa* and encountered the first ghostly phenomenon. Back home *Soham* becomes critical and was pained by the spirit. At a critical juncture, *Dr Nachiketa* turns up at the house of *Dr.Chatterjee* and saves *Soham* from the evil spirit. Then *Dr Nachiketa* finds the reason behind the spirit's haunting after *Soham* and performs the rituals to liberate the evil spirit. The story influences

Dr Sen. At home *Soumi*, the daughter of *Dr Sen* starts behaving strangely at nights. She becomes a lost girl who is always attracted to the foggy garden. *Dr Sen* and his wife finds that some dark shadows from the garden are trying to take their daughter into the garden. They make every effort to save their daughter but their every effort becomes futile. At last at a dire situation, *Dr Sen* decides to contact *Dr Chatterjee* for the assistance of *Dr.Nachiketa*. *Dr Nachiketa* promptly arrives and makes out what the problem is. He shows everyone about the access of the Dark Spirits in the garden and inside the house. *Dr.Nachiketa* explains their garden to be the portal to another realm which gives access to the entities of the other world. He explains how *Soumi's* consciousness is trapped in that world. He arranges an astral experience for everyone and himself goes into that dark world to save *Soumi's* inner self. He encounters a lot of the dark shadows but eventually saves *Soumi*.

THE MYSTERIOUS PATIENT

Dr Sen checked his wristwatch. It was a quarter past four in the afternoon. His clinic at his house starts at 5 p.m. Pleasant winter sun rays through his car glass relieved him from biting cold. January winter at *Kalimpong* is really unbearable. He was lost in his own contemplation. He even did not want to look at the other friends and parents who turned up to pick up their children. The gate of *St. Augustine's School* is now crowded. It would take hardly thirty minutes more for the darkness to envelope the whole area. The whole day had been dull with fog and biting wind. This ephemeral sunshine turned up to be a bounty of nature and everyone found those favoured places where sun bestowed its soothing but slanting streaks. However, *Dr Sen* could not drink in the healing weather as a mental uneasiness made him sore. He is not at the peak of his mental tranquillity and searching the reason he could not sum up anything else but his daughter.

Soumi, his sixteen-year-old daughter is a girl of attraction now. She is five feet six with a slender frame. Her cute smile on a babyface with physical developments made her look like an angel. Everything was on the swift state for her. But in the last three weeks, she has become different. The first reason that *Dr Sen* thought was this new place with a limited number of friends and neighbours. But this concern was found irrelevant on finding the arrival of a lot of school friends at their home.

The thought of his home gave him little ease. *The Seventh Heaven* was really a matter of good luck to him. It was beyond his expectation to be the owner of such a house at a very cheap rate. The house was crafted with care and taste. The ground floor is furnished with a library, a hall and an attached room leading to the main entrance. The veranda is long and big. The first floor is with three-bedrooms and two other small rooms. The most fascinating part of the house was, of course, the balcony on the first floor. Every bedroom had a balcony in the North. The balcony is invigorating and soothing because it opens to a splendid garden. The garden is well planned and decorated with all sorts of flower plants, fruits trees and other elegant decorative trees. The garden merges with the hilly slopes and the natural forest land.

The last bell of the school brought him back to his senses. He could see *Soumi,* his angel with lost vigour. He was sad and irritated with her nowadays. She has developed annoyance with rough behaviour. The agile, naughty, ever-smiling girl now keeps always dejected and irritated. *Soumi* with a dull face opened the door and sat in the back of the car.

Dr Sen asked, “How was your day dear?”

She did not think of answering. She stared outside. *Dr Sen* decided to move as his clinic starts at five. The car moved on the windy hilly roads. Startled with a gust *Dr Sen* looked at *Soumi* who had brought the glass of the car window down allowing icy cold wind in. *Dr Sen* restrained himself from saying anything as the car reached the house gate.

Soumi entered and took out a chips packet and sat on the sofa switching the T.V. on. This time *Dr Sen* could not contain himself. With an angry tone, he said, "*Soumi*, behave yourself, you should change your school uniform and then get to other things".

As if heard nothing, she kept on watching T.V.

This time *Dr Sen* acted with irritation and anger. Out of sudden impulse, he switched the T.V. off. At this *Soumi* stood up and without uttering a single word went upstairs.

Contrary to his nature *Dr Sen* went furious and shouted at her saying, "Do not be so adamant, life is not so easy. Learn to be a modest girl. I won't tolerate.........."

Dr Sen could not finish as his better half *Soumali Sen* entered. She is elegant in look. At her middle age, even she has an appeal for anyone who beholds her for the first time. Keeping her bag on the sofa she said, "Let me talk, shouting at her won't do any good." She went upstairs into *Soumi's* room.

SOUL-THE DEBATE

The advent of a lot of patients in the clinic helped *Dr Sen* to forget everything about *Soumi*. Dr Sen called for *Sanjana. Sanjana Dorji* is a sweet *Nepali* girl who looks after the work of listing the names of the patients and maintaining them. She speaks fluent Bengali and *Dr Sen* has never seen a calm and beautiful girl with dark eyes and hair like her among the Nepalese. *Sanjana* came and said, "Yes Doctor."

"Give me a cup of coffee. And how many are there?"

"Five more left Doctor."

Sipping coffee *Dr Sen* felt rejuvenated. He checked the time. It was almost seven p.m. He will go to *Dr Majumdar's* house. He eagerly waits for this period of the day. He forgets every worry there. A few other doctors gather there and they enjoy gossiping. Thinking about going there *Dr Sen* got charged up and shouted, "*Sanjana* send the next". Covered with blanket one middle-aged person entered.

Dr Sen asked--"What is your name?"

- After a while with effort, the person uttered "*Manab*"

- *Dr Sen* looked at him. He was trembling. Only his eyes, nose and a part of the mouth could be seen.

Dr Sen asked, "What happened?"

-"*Babu,* fever," he answered in a trembling voice.

- *Dr Sen* was bewildered to find his high temperature. With a surprise, he asked, "How could you come to my place? You are burning out from fever."

Manab's eyes were very red. In a low voice *Manab* answered, "*Babu* my body did not want but when you are with a rebel mind, body complies."

Dr Sen was taken aback to hear such words from an illiterate person. Out of curiosity, he asked-"What are you?"

With an effort in half whispering voice, he said-

"-*Babu* I am just a flower trader. The garden that is attached to your house, I stay North-East of that garden."

At this *Dr, Sen* pondered and thought to use this opportune moment and stated- "My garden is filled with fruits and flower trees and coincidentally I am in search of a gardener to look after my garden."

After a short pause *Dr Sen* continued "If you are with a bit of time, I would like to engage you for my garden. I shall see that you are paid enough."

Suddenly with protruding eyes, the man uttered in one breath-

"Your garden….your garden does not require any caretaker. Your garden is not yours any more. It had never been yours. It had never belonged to anybody. There are a lot who control your garden. None can enter the garden without their permission. The Seventh Heaven is nothing but the big living Hell."

"But I did not engage anybody to take care of my garden," with a surprise *Dr Sen* stated.

With crimson red-eye again he said – "They do not want your consent. They own the garden from long. Time, nature, birth and death everything is futile there. Darkness reigns there."

Now it was certain for *Dr Sen* that the man was an insane. He tried to avoid the matter of the garden. He asked him to show his tongue. *Dr Sen* thought that excessive fever might have disturbed his mental equilibrium and hence he is talking nonsense.

While checking his tongue suddenly the shawl got removed from his face and the view of his right cheek made *Dr Sen* shiver. His right cheek is sore and he could clearly see the mark of four fingers. As if a maniac has burnt his cheek with red hot iron fingers. The injury has turned into a sore.

Dr Sen was perplexed asked- "How did it happen?"

- "I am punished. I am punished for illegal intrusion."
- "What?"
- "Nothing *Doctor Babu*. Wait for the opportune time. The mist will clear away. You won't need any explanation then. Goodbye *Doctor Babu.*"
- Thinking for a while *Dr Sen* said-
- "Wait, take these medicines. You'll be all right."
- "Medicine can't cure *Doctor Babu*. This pain and suffering is nothing to what pain caused to me by those sounds and sights."

Then suddenly turning and leaning on the table of the *Doctor* with his red eye and dirty bearded face he said –

"*Doctor Babu*, disbelief can only be removed by experience. When the world of dark turns up to you in a most unexpected manner, you turn bewildered and insane. We do not wait for something but they wait for you and you have no way to escape your fate."

Uttering these words he abruptly went out.

Dr Sen looked at the door through which he disappeared but did not want to waste his time in the words of the lunatic.

ILLNESS OF SOHAM AND THE FIRST GHOSTLY EXPERIENCE

Dr Sen reached *Dr Majumder's* house a bit late. Since afternoon he could not erase the words of *Manab.* His words as if cannot summarily be the words of a good-for-nothing. When he reached *Dr Majumder's* house, already *Dr Kumar*, *Dr Dey* and *Dr Chatterjee* were in the middle of a dcbate.

Seeing *Dr, Sen*, *Dr Dey* asked him "Here *Dr Sen* answer me a question",

-"Yes"

-"*Dr Chatterjee* says that soul exists scientifically. He is giving the reference to *Dr MacDougall's* example. *Dr MacDougall* had measured the weight of the soul and it was 21 gram. Now tell me, being a man of science can you accept this?"

-"No, not certainly. But at the same time, we need to know the detail of his opinion.

-"Well, we have debated a lot. You would not debate with me if you met *Dr Nachiketa*," *Dr Chatterjee* looked calm and sane.

-"Who is he and what is he?" asked *Dr Dey*.

-"To tell about him always words fall short. He is the famous paranormal specialist who has been meant as an institution. World-famous psychiatrists consider his vast knowledge as unfathomable. He is the one who has transcended all the dimensions of the human mind and the ghostly world. And moreover, this is not hearsay, rather my personal experience. Coincidentally and I would say for me luckily I met him in a most unexpected situation where my profession had done everything resulting in nothing but futility. My family is in perfect health and happiness and *Dr Nachiketa* is the only reason for this."

Dr Dey got up and keeping his right hand on the shoulder of *Dr Chatterjee* said-

"You must understand the psychology. When we are in fear of losing, we cling to the spiritual aspects and if get anything positive out of it coincidentally, we turn blind believing it. But I do not count you with the common God fanatics and as I know you very closely, I would like to hear your experience."

Dr Chatterjee took off his Monel metal frame spectacle, kept it on the table and looking up to the opposite window started-

"Well this is not a story made hyperbolic or fabricated. I am connected to this true incident and my only son *Soham* is with me today beyond the realm of all reasons.

Two years before I was posted in *Siliguri* and was enjoying every happiness of family life. *Soham* was then four years old. His presence was like the sweet morning sunshine to us. Both I and my wife *Sushmita* were blessed to have such an angel in our lives. His innocuous words, infantile activities always made us forget all drudgery. But this happy heavenly state was under an evil eye.

I still remember the day. It was the second day of *Kali Puja*. We were all tired of attending friends' and relatives' houses. So after we had returned home, we were fast asleep. That night around two my wife discovered *Soham* was not on the bed. We searched for him and found in the adjacent room sitting near a wardrobe. He was crying there silently. The house we used to stay was a rented one. The house was spacious but a bit demoded one. He was staring fixedly at the base of the wardrobe. His eyes were in tears. We brought him back on the bed. He was still in tears. We asked him a lot. He did not utter a word. He was disturbed that night.

Next day I left the house in the very fine morning for an emergency call. Around morning eleven my wife called me informing about the high fever of *Soham*. When I reached home at around two pm, *Soham* was really suffering. I checked his temperature and gave him an Acetaminophen and waited.

Around three we were having our lunch. We were shocked to see *Soham* standing near us in a daze. *Sushmita* was anxious. She rushed to him and was bewildered touching his body. He was burning. I did not delay. Within an hour I admitted him in the hospital. I hope you remember *Dr Abraham*, my friend, he attended him and was shocked to find him continuing with hundred and five fever and still talking and behaving normally.

However, next afternoon, *Soham* recovered. But he was not my little lamb any more. His kiddish pranks, prancing like a colt around the home, his trains, cars, helicopters, everything turned black and white. He was always silent, as if in a hypnotised state. He no longer giggled watching *Motu Patlu* and *Chota Bheem*. He just stared at everything and hardly responded. What increased our worry was his dislike for the food.

Within seven days his condition made us go mad. My wife a preacher of modern Science began worshipping. I did not follow her. I had to save my son. I decided to go for a better diagnosis. I booked immediate available tickets for *Chennai Apollo Hospital.* Thinking about the three-day-long journey to *Chennai* was killing us from inside.

Soham's deteriorating health made me forget everything happening around. Food, work, T V, people, everything turned futile. On 20th November, we boarded on the train to *Kolkata.* We had our flights booked for Chennai from *Dumdum Airport.* We boarded on the *Kanchan Kanya Express* to reach *Kolkata.* It was night and I was a bit allayed as we started off at last. We got our seats in the middle and lower berth. *Soham* was like apparent asymptomatic. It was hard to find any effect of his declining health on him.

With us, there were two *Marwaries* travelling. They had their bookings at the opposite of our berths. They came into the compartment with their unintelligible tongue. One of them pronounced about their tickets booked for middle and upper berth. Then they secured their seats at the lower berth. The man who was to be there at the lower berth was yet to turn up.

When the train reached *New Jalpaiguri Junction* around quarter past eight at night, the man meant for the lower berth showed up. He was tall with a sharp nose and regular haircut. With searching eyes behind the short rimmed spectacle, he adjusted his luggage and sat with the newspapers. He barely lifted his head out of the newspapers. He looked calm and composed. *The Marwaris* were conversing in *Hindi* with their accent. I did not understand their topic of discussion. I was looking at *Soham* who was lying on her mother's lap.

My heart sank when I discovered the nails of *Soham.* The nails were ash black. Without uttering a single word, I showed his nails to *Sushmita.* Her dejection doubled up and she started to sob. One of the *Marwaris* noticed and asked-

"What happened?"

I made them understand that my son was sick and we were moving for medical solutions. Now the man opposite lifted his head, folded the newspaper, took out his thermos flask and began drinking coffee perhaps. He seemed to me to be unfriendly one.

At that moment another man entered. His oily hair turned back, red *tilak* on the forehead and the big handlebar moustache made his appearance a bit horrifying one. He checked his berth and dumped his luggage on the upper berth. He sat beside us, opened his water bottle and started to drink water from it. He looked at *Soham* and said-

"What happened to the boy? He looks unhealthy".

Both I and my wife went silent. My wife looked at me and then told about *Soham's* sickness. We were rather embarrassed talking about *Soham's* sickness. The man with dilated eyes approached slowly towards *Soham.* All were transfixed and curious about what he would do next. He held the hand of

Soham and at once shook off and uttered -*"Oom Namah Shivay"*.

He kept looking at the boy for a few seconds and slowly turned his head towards us and said, "My name is *Upendranath Sharma*. I am an astrologer and a master in *Tantric* healing." The man sitting opposite now took his head up and glanced *at Upendranath Sharma*. Then he lowered his eyes down.

Upendranath Sharma then said, "Allow me to check his pulse. I could not stop him. He looked at his watch feeling the pulse. Then he checked *Soham's* eyes and looked at his nails. His brow tightened and checked the nails with utmost intentness. Then slowly he wavered his hand around his naval area and suddenly lifted his hand as if he received an electric shock. Then he again moved his hand towards his neck and then held his index finger in the middle of *Soham's* eyebrows. He kept his finger in the middle of the eyebrows for a few seconds, then slowly looked down and with a pale and withered face. He asked me-

"How many days has your son been with the dark nails?"

Reflecting in the past *Sushmita* said, "We have noticed his black nails today, in fact just thirty minutes before."

The two *Marwaries* were staring at us. The man opposite us was busy with his book. *Upendranath Sharma* continued-

"I do not know whether you believe in the other world or not …."

He could not finish his words as the man opposite to us closed the book with a thud, changed the position of the legs and looked at *Soham.* All looked at him and *Upendranath Sharma* resumed,-

"I mean, I think your son is not going to be cured by medical means."

My wife lifted her head with a perturbed look and asked, “What do you mean? Tell us clearly.”

-“See often people face sudden unexpected troubles in lives and we blame to fate. We do so because we really do not have any explanation behind the unexpected and unwanted trouble. I am sure that you do not know any reason behind his sickness. He is in high fever but did he catch a cold? Or did you find any viral attack or any mosquito induced reason?”

Upendranath stared with his logics. My scientific belief and my profession made me feel irritated with this kind of hoax person. I retorted-

“I am sorry sir, I do not believe in something that you are hinting at. I am sure that my child is going through a physical issue which is possible to solve medically and we are moving to a better place where we shall get things fixed in a scientific way.”

Upendranath seemed a bit taken aback and pressing his hands together he said-

"Of course you can try medical ways. But your scientific fix is not going to do any good to your son. Your son is possessed. And by the time you will experiment your medical ways, your son will transcend the line, and bringing him back will be impossible then. Slowly the thing is eating him away. His black nails and drowsy pale eyes suggest that you have less time. I am *Upendranath Sharma*, I am from *Banaras*. Remember, I am not after money. We, the healers are vowed for healing without benefits. If you really want your son to be fine and normal again change your decision as quickly as possible."

Sushmita asked," What has happened to my son?"

I interrupted her and said, "Do not believe his words. We shall get him cured."

Sushmita cast an irritating eye on me and asked again-

"Please tell us what has happened to my son"?

Upendranath pondered a bit and said-

"I am not sure but things indicate that your son is possessed by a spirit which has possessed your son out of an unfulfilled desire in the mortal life. But the symptoms suggest that the spirit is not here to stay in his body for his unfulfilled desire but the spirit wants your son permanently in his world. Coming full moon your son must be put through a series of rituals to force the spirit to leave him. I am an expert in energy healing. If think that you need me, here is my card. Call and reach my place."

I was listening to his nonsense talks and could not take it anymore and retorted, "Listen *Mr.Upendranath*, my son is not possessed and if you think my son is possessed then prove it now."

The man sitting opposite to us lifted his head with a searching eye and the two *Marwaries* were looking very much excited.

Upendranath Sharma looked at me and then looked at others and said, "Well as you wish. But this may turn your son violent."

-"I do not care because I know that my son is not possessed."

-"That's fine. I shall require one lemon, a little bit of sea salt and one glass. I shall attempt two ways and in both the ways you will find the presence of a spirit in your son's body."

Immediately the two *Marwaries* got involved as the things were now turning interesting. One of the *Marwaris* took out a few lemons and handed it out to *Mr Upendranath.*

As if charged up with confidence *Mr Upendranath* took one of the lemons. Another *Marwari* stopped a moving tea vendor and asked for salt. Now the ingredients required for the process were at the hand of *Mr Upendranath*.

He kept his bag on the lower berth and took out a few of the materials. He took out three hexagonal copper containers. Then he rubbed his both palms for a few seconds and then lifted the shirt of *Soham* and opened his tummy bare. His milky white soft tummy with the naval was exposed. *Upendranath* moved his hand around his tummy and then opened one of his copper boxes.

Sushmita once looked at me with a worried face. I was even feeling awkward as I allowed this man to perform his insane works with my son. However, I kept quiet. From the first box, he took out crimson powder and put it around the naval of *Soham.* Normally *Soham* giggles if anyone touches his tummy even if he is asleep. But now he was quiet with his eyes closed. *Upendranath* carefully perfected the circle. Then he opened another box and opened turmeric powder. He made another circle with the turmeric powder outside the first circle. Now he opened the third box and took out a vial container filled with some liquid. It looked a little yellowish. Now he slowly opened it. At this moment he started chanting some mantras. Then chanting the mantra he dropped three drops of the liquid in the naval of *Soham*. Now he said, "Within ten minutes the liquid will turn black. And if it happens, then surely your son is possessed by the evil one."

I stopped him in the middle and said, "Where is the connection of the liquid's turning black to that of my son's being possessed by the evil spirit?"

Upendranath said, "The liquid is of the holy water of the *Ganges* and has been energized with certain rituals which repel the evil spirits. The crimson powder and the turmeric powder create a strong positive field which forces the spirit to show its true nature by turning the water black"

I said, "I do not believe, but let's see."

Then *Upendranath* cut the lemon into two pieces and took one piece and mixed with it crimson and turmeric powder. Then he took out a small packet from his bag in which there was ash kept. He took a pinch of ash and put it in the middle of the eyebrow of *Soham*. Then he held the lemon piece in the middle of *Soham's* eyebrow and started chanting a mantra.

Suddenly *Mr Upendranath* started to shake. There was no effect on *Soham*. He was lying in a dazed state without any moil. The two *Marwaries* were transfixed as they were under the effect of adrenaline. I stood up puzzled. Then within a moment concluded this to be a pretending behaviour to make us believe that this was the work of the ghost that was within *Soham*. Before I could say him something, the man sitting opposite stood up and kept his hand on the back of *Mr Upendranath*. He kept his hand on the back of him until *Updendranath* was fine. I realized that the man was pressing his index finger at a certain point of the spine.

Mr Upendranath turned with bewildered state and asked, "Who are you?"

The man said, "You have enough time to know about me, but you must correct the mistakes that you did."

"What mistakes are you talking about?"

"At first chant the correct *Sabara Mantra*. You were chanting opposite, so you were under the effect of the process. *Sabara Mantra* must be used with precision because these mantras are very strong in nature from their inceptions."

Mr Upendranath at this started to chant the mantra again touching the forehead of *Soham* with the lemon. But as he started, again he messed with the mantra and started to tremble.

The man now removed *Upendranath's* hand and held his own hand on the forehead of *Soham* and chanted with an impressive tone-

Sarasvatī gāḍī sunna kā dīyā rupē kī bātī guṇa bātī bātī. Aṅkīnī, ḍaṅkīnī, śaṅkhinī, jādū ṭōnā mērī bhavānī isī ghaḍī yahām̐ sē nikala jāya, mērī ȧāna mērē gurū kī ȧāna īśvara gaurā pārvatī mahādēva kī duhā'ī.

And then he carried the lemon from the nose of *Soham* up to his naval. When the lemon reached naval *Soham's* eyes shot up and he kicked *Mr Updendrath.Upendranath* fell on to the side lower berth horrified. Then *Soham* looked at the man and held his throat with his two tiny hands. The man held his thumb finger on the forehead of *Soham* and within a moment *Soham* fell silent and went to sleep. The man returned to his berth. The two *Marwaries* were now with dried throat looking horrifyingly at each other.

Upendranath gathered himself with effort and coming back to his place looked at *Soham,* then me and my wife and then at the man. After a short pause, He said, "I hope now you are sure of the possession of the spirit on your son."

I said, "What I saw now is nothing but hysterics. My son reacted in this way because of your nonsensical activities on his body."

Sushmita was in tears. She spoke nothing and was gazing at *Soham.*

The man said now in the gravest voice, "*Doctor*, your son is possessed. You are a man of science, but the phenomenon of the other world is not to be summarily rejected".

"I can understand that you are also an accomplice with this knave and your aim is to thug the people who are in utmost penury", I said in a sarcastic tone.

The man smiled and said, "This is not your mistake *Doctor*. Your experience with many of the thugs made you believe this. But at the same time remember the fact that people get their faith eternally when they despise it the most. Your son is possessed and you can try medical ways that will subdue the problem, but it cannot do away with the reason."

Now *Mr Upendranath* spoke out, "How did you save me from the repel of the *Stambhan* on me. My Guru does not indulge in ghost driving after he had a strong repel of *Stambhan*.

"If you have proper control over the energies, then repulsive *Stambhan* can be stopped."

"As per my knowledge, not many are there with the ability to repel it. Who are you?"

"My name is *Dr Nachiketa Banerjee*. People call me popularly as Doctor".

"Oh my God! *Dr Nachiketa*? I-I am privileged to have a meeting with you. You are the institution. Your example is given in teaching tantric philosophy".

Then looking at me *Upendranath* said, "Doctor if he wishes he can cure your son right now. You are lucky to have a person travelling with you."

The two *Marwaries* were staring at us and the other two in a puzzle.

"But still now I am not certain of your demand. I did not get assured that my son is possessed. Curing him is the next question." I was rigid at my point.

Dr Nachiketa looked at me and said with a smiling face, "*Dr Chatterjee* when this kind of ritual is performed spirits do not stay inside the body for some moments so that they can perform the repulsive attack on the healer. The same mistake is done by *Mr, Upendranath.* During the initiation of the ritual, he must have used *Bandhan* ritual to trap the spirit so that the spirit could be forced to leave the body permanently. But now the most interesting fact is that after I used the driving energy in your Son's body the spirit or I must say spirts have come out of your son's body to try for a repulsive attack on me, but still, they did not get any chance because I have higher aura protection and they have realized that I can move to their world and can finish them permanently."

"These are nothing but the words of swanking. Your words are mere words and do not satisfy my question"

"*Dr Nachiketa* lifted his hand and said, "Wait a moment *Doctor*, I am going to satisfy you to the utmost."

Now *Dr Nachiketa* stood up and nearing the window suddenly removed the curtains into one side and blew hot air from within his mouth which made the window smoky. And immediately all could see two white fishy eyes, with a whitish face at the back of the window staring. *Sushmita* shrilled and all others were gaping at the sight with complete horror. Slowly the face faded away in the darkness.

“Haha ha”, *Dr Nachiketa* laughed aloud and looked at everybody.

“I have never seen a spirit in such a concentrated form like this and so horrible!” Said *Mr Upendranath* in a real panic.

The two *Marwaries* were now visibly in perspiration and was unable to say anything.

I do not know what happened to me. I was still in the mode of refuting. I said, “We—ll, I would say that you can make others believe in your illusions, but I am not going to believe that what we visualized was really something of a spirit.”

Listening this *Dr.Nachiketa* stopped for a while and said, “See *Dr Chatterjee*, I am not an illusionist, neither am I a magician. In real sense to explain me to you is a bit tough. I love to believe myself as a tiny creature crawling in different dimensions. Normally I do not persuade people like you to believe on me, but as we are bound to be together for at least for a few hours let me try to make you feel that I am at least not a liar. Give me your hands.”

I stretched my hands which *Dr Nachiketa* held and looked down closing his eyes. Then looking at me he said, “Your wife is not the first lady who is in your life.” Saying this he looked at me. Luckily he was right and moreover I was lucky that I had told about this to my wife.

I said, “This is a common guess.”

“There were three times in your life that you feel yourself to be guilty for the death of three people whom you should have saved. One eleven-year-old boy, one middle-aged serviceman and an old lady.”

This was what that something shook me. I had never shared this secret with anyone, not even my wife. I did not utter a word and he continued-

"Your son *Soham* had come into your life before your marriage".

And this made me and my wife gaped. We had successfully kept this secret from everyone until today. We had been physically intimate before our marriage. As a result here came *Soham*. To keep this a secret we got married. I realized that he is a man of some occult knowledge. So I took my hands off and looked at *Soham.*

There was a bit of pause as I had withdrawn myself .*Mr. Upendranath* sighed a breath of relief as he felt his demands at least proved perfect with a proper presentation.

My wife was sobbing and she had an air of dejection.

At this *Dr, Nachiketa* broke his silence and said, "*Mrs Chaterjee*, angels make mistake, humans make mistake, but devils never make mistakes. They never get deviated from their target. A devil is destroyed by a devilish pretention."

Sushmita looked up and with folded hands requested, "Please tell us how we can save our son "?

"Well, *Dr, Chatterjee* is still with a desire to go for medical ways. Let your husband try for his satisfaction. Till then wash your son every dusk with saltwater and feed him lemon water kept in inside a conch for the whole night. Just maintain this for the days you are going to be there in for medication. You will get conches in Burra Bazar in Kolkata."

Sushmita looked at me for a few seconds and then said, "I shall make sure that it is done with precision".

To ease the situation *Dr Nachiketa* said, "Would you like some coffee, I have some nice coffee with me."

I nodded and in two minutes we were sipping coffee. And there had been discussions about some other topics.

Around nine-thirty *Mr Upendranath* got down at the *Kishanganj* station. He was beaming with the satisfaction of having met *Dr, Nachiketa.*

Around eleven forty *Dr Nachiketa* got up and bade goodbye. *Sushmita* got up and said, "If we really need you, in our dire situation, how can we contact?"

Dr Nachiketa smiled and pointed to a paper he kept on the seat as if he was very sure that we shall have to come to him for the saving of our son. He left with a smile at *Barsoi Junction.*

The Paper had only two things written-

Doctor and underneath that his phone number.

DOCTOR NACHIKETA SAVES SOHAM

My wife started to follow the ways stated by *Dr Nachiketa* and I did not refute. We were en route to *Chennai Apollo* but slowly I started to feel the religious way to be the ultimate way. However, we reached *Chennai* Apollo. The group of doctors diagnosed him concluded nothing serious about his health. They rather stated *Soham* to suffer from *hepatoma* that might have caused due to psychic trauma. We were advised to consult a psychiatrist. We did not want any stone to be unturned. So we consulted the best psychiatrist of *Apollo*. He prescribed some medicines and he surmised that *Soham* should be right within a month.

We left from *Chennai* without getting to any concrete reason behind *Soham's* sickness. *Sushmita* followed the instructions of *Dr Nachiketa* and *Soham* did not deteriorate any further. He did not have a fever or any other complications anymore. But his nails remained black and he did not revive to his innocuous and lively state. We were not at peace of mind because we knew that *Soham* was not fully fine. However, I waited for the medicine to work and to see everything to be normal again.

But things turned other ways. One December afternoon I was on the sofa watching T V. Suddenly *Sushmita* called me in the bedroom. *Soham* was sleeping in there. I was anxious that something might have happened wrong. I rushed in and found *Sushmita* pointing at something. I looked carefully and noticed that from one the nostrils of *Soham* there was a thin lock of hair coming out. I checked the hair carefully and discovered that the hair was not of *Soham*, rather the hair was of any woman. I pulled the hair lock and to my surprise, the hair lock came out almost a feet out of the nostril of *Soham. Soham* seemed to be in a trance and not in his senses. I was about to check the hair carefully and then I could feel a pull from inside. As if someone was pulling the hair lock. Then with a sudden pull, the hair slipped back inside the nostril of *Soham. Sushmita* was sobbing deeply and even I could not understand the very reason behind this. I knew with every passing incident my scientific mind was getting weaker. I checked the nostril of *Soham* carefully but found nothing.

That night we sat on the bed near *Soham* sleeping. We had less conversation and more sighs. We had no focus on the chores of the house. At around night eleven I was dozing and *Sushmita* had her eyes on *Soham*. She had been crying her eyes out since we have returned from Chennai.

Around night one *Sushmita* shook me fervently. I was in utmost shock. I got up and asked her the reason for calling in such a way. She pointed me something towards *Soham*. I could not see anything particular. Then *Shusmita* removed the quilt of *Soham* a bit and I could not believe my eyes what I saw. Little tiny fingers of *Soham* were held by the hand of a woman. I marked properly and realized that the hand was actually holding *Soham's* hand from the back of the bedpost. The hand looked fair with nail polish and bangles. As I moved nearer the hand slowly released the hand of *Soham* and disappeared back of the bedpost. *Sushmita* fainted on the bed. I brought water and revived the consciousness of *Sushmita.* She looked horrible and with a shuddering voice she said, "What was that?" Then suddenly changing her face into a serious one said, "I want my son to be fine at anyway. Tomorrow you will call *Dr, Nachiketa.* It is only he who can save *Soham.* I do not want to listen to anything from you. Nothing is more important than the life of my son"

I said, "Yes, I shall call. Now please try to sleep a bit. Come just sleep a bit."

She had put *Soham* in the middle of two of us. She held *Soham* tightly at her bosom. However, I could not sleep. I even inspected the bedpost and found nothing. I took the mobile and thought to talk. Then restrained myself as it was already night twelve. I sent a text message in his number stating his help that we need badly.

At around night four I slept. I had a dream where I could see the whole incident being repeated. In the dream, I saw ourselves sleeping as we had been sleeping. Then I noticed the woman's hand holding *Soham's* hand. Slowly I could see the blurred shape of the woman standing near the bedpost of *Soham.* She was clad in a red saree. She had a slender body. I tried to see her face but I could not. The horrifying deed she started. She started lifting *Soham* with her hands. And the next moment I could see the back of the lady carrying *Soham* out of the room. I tried to shout but could not utter a single word. I could see the lady going out of the room door which ushered in intense white light. I felt weak all over and was dejected and defeated and lost. I started to wail as I felt that I lost *Soham* forever. Then looked at *Sushmita* lying on the bed with an ashen face. I could not bear the possibility of losing *Soham.* I lifted myself with full effort and dragged myself out of the door and saw the lady walking through the fog out of the main door of the house. I shouted after her,

“Stop”. Suddenly the lady stopped. Then the lady turned herself sideways slowly and through the fog. I could see the lax body of *Soham* on her hands. She looked at me momentarily and again started walking. I tried to run after but could not. I was numb all over. I fell down. I could see her translucent legs moving ahead. Through the fog, she was getting lost. Tears rolled down from my eyes. Suddenly she stopped just before the main gate. Through her translucent body, I could see a figure standing out of the gate. She hesitated and took a few wobbling steps backwards. There was a man approaching through the main gate. His gait and dress seemed to be known. Through the fog came he. Slowly the lady turned jittery. She dropped *Soham* and demobilized into the fog. The man slowly came, lifted *Soham* and approached towards me. As he came near I recognized him for he was *Dr Nachiketa.* Suddenly I jumped off on the bed and looked for *Soham*. He was not there. I heard voices outside. *Sushmita* got up. We stared at each other as that was the babbling of *Soham* outside in the yard. We rushed off to the garden and found *Soham* running after his favourite red ball and he looked vibrant and healthy. I knew that *Soham* is back and fine. For a moment I thought I was dreaming. Then we found Dr *Nachiketa* sitting on the concrete block of the stairs. *Sushmita* could not believe her eyes. She rushed and embraced *Soham* with utmost emotion. With gratitude and obeisance, I went *to Dr Nachiketa* and held his hands. He smiled and said

"*Soham* is fine now. The lady cannot take him anymore."

With shock and amazement, I asked, "What I dreamt just a while ago, was it true?"

"Yes, true of course. You can see your son as you wanted to see him."

I was puzzled and asked him, "It is all mysterious to me how you could save *Soham*. I mean how did you do this in the dream."?

In the meantime, *Sushmita* stood near us with *Soham* in a deep caress.

"It was the dream created by the lady so that she could take *Soham* with her. Her main purpose was to make you weak in the dream. She chose to do this in the dream of you because she is the stronger one in the dream than you are. She is not strong enough to do this in real life. It would take her time to do this. The process would have been slow and time-consuming. "

"You mean that she really took *Soham* away? I mean did she do that in dream or reality?"

"She did this in reality but she made you conscious about this in your dream so that your effort to stop her will never be possible. In your dream, you are rather a very helpless one who even does not have control over himself. So protecting your son in that realm was impossible for you."

Sushmita was looking at us in complete amazement. Then she shook herself and stated –

“ *Dr Nachiketa*, please come inside. While walking in she looked back at *Dr Nachiketa* and said – “ Now I know that my son will be fine”.Immediately she corrected herself and said, “Actually he is already fine and I know it well that you have done this .”

“ He is fine. There is no doubt about this but *Soham* is not safe yet. The entity which had almost been successful will be back in other ways and we have to make sure that it never happens.”

That day *Dr Nachiketa* moved around the house. We showed him the place near the wall wardrobe where we had first discovered *Soham* in a dazed state.

In the afternoon *Dr Nachiketa* sitting on the sofa called *Soham* who was at his highest mirth with his bicycle. His BSA Champ cycle was his most favourite. He came prancing and sat near the *Doctor*. *Dr, Nachiketa* took *Soham's* both hands in his hands and immediately there was a change in the pallor of *Soham*. He kept quiet as if he had been put into a trance. *Dr Nachiketa* held his hands closing his eyes for a minute and then spoke, "*Mrs Chaterjee, Soham's* nails have gone big. Why don't you cut them?" The doctor looked at *Sushmita* as if he wanted this to be done now. *Sushmita* brought the nail cutter and started to trim the nails of *Soham. Dr Nachiketa* took all of *Soham's* black nails and kept on the glass coffee table kept in the middle of the sofas.

Then *Dr Nachiketa* took his mobile out and called. He had a short conversation.
"Hello, *Pragya*?

-"Where are you?"

-"Take a taxi and reach at the address that I have texted you. And did you bring the things I have told you?"

"Ok..ok."

"Is there anybody coming?" I asked surmising the conversation.

Dr Nachiketa answered, "*Pragya*, my assistant is on the way to your house. She is with some of the things that I require to complete the task here."

THE SPIRIT OF THE WOMAN

After half an hour a taxi stopped at the front gate. One girl of about twenty-five got out of the car. She was milky white in complexation with curled thick hair and a square spectacle. She looked awesomely attractive. When she approached us she looked five feet and six with perfect and appealing curves. She smiled at us with cute dimples on two sides. She carried a big brown tourist bag. She entered and handed the bag to *Dr Nachiketa.*

"Doctor you did not inform that you are here so far in *Siliguri*. I had to cancel a get together with my old friends."

Dr. kept the bag on the floor and suddenly turned and said to us, "Well I forgot to tell you. This is *Pragya Acharya*, my caretaker. She is a PhD in parapsychology from the USA. She is very talented and brave. Without her, I am a lame man."

"Doctor you are using all honeyed words. Talking tall about me will not make me something great. I am a microbe to what you are and perhaps I shall not be able to reach your attainment in my whole lifetime."

"Well let's get back to work.

-"*Pragya* half of this room should be filled a centimetre with water now. Remember this time it should be tonic water and the North part of the room."

I asked "Tonic water? And what is the use of tonic water here?"

"You know *Dr. Chaterjee* tonic water is rich with quinine and it will allow us to see what we cannot see in the dark. I have a suspicion and I shall check the fact to be sure about the source."

As a doctor, I knew that tonic water is actually used against malaria and it is bitter in taste. Nowadays people even demand this tonic water to be effective for diabetes. I was thinking over this when *Pragya* asked showing a bucket full of water, "Doctor how many bottles should I use here?"

Dr Nachiketa pondered a bit and then answered. "Four bottles will do but first make sure that half the room is well protected".

Pragya is intelligent. It took her half an hour to make me arrange wooden pieces, plastic and M-seal to make half the room waterproof.

Doctor was on the sofa watching everything .after the work was over he said, "Take the video cameras and make sure that the whole room is covered well. We shall start exactly after 9 pm."

Up to nine pm, we had a hearty time spent where Doctor *Nachiketa* seemed none other than a common man. We had hearty dinner and he advised us to make *Soham* sleep in his bedroom with his mother.

After *Soham* slept Dr. went to his bedroom and cut a bunch of hair from *Sushmita* and tied it in the little fingers of her and *Soham*".

I did not ask anything as I did not want to interfere with his work. You can better say I had a deep faith in the ability of *Dr Nachiketa.*

Around nine pm Doctor asked *Pragya* to turn on the cameras. While *Pragya* was turning on the cameras, he took the bucket of water and poured in four bottles of tonic water into the bucket, stirred it well and then from one corner slowly poured the water on the floor and waited for the water to reach every corner of the area.

At around, eleven night Doctor took out a small paper packet. He had the cut nails of *Soham*. What he intended was beyond my thought. I decided to wait and be patient. He told me to turn the lights off. I turned all the lights off and at once the whole room turned bright neon blue as tonic water started to glow in the darkness.

Doctor now sat on his toes and mixed the nails with crimson powder with the chanting '*Om Kham*

Brahm" for a few times and dropped a few nails of *Soham* and waited.

I could not believe my eyes what happened next. From the nails started a flow of black water. It moved in different directions and stopped in the centre of the watered area and then moved to the North-Eastern corner of the room and rested right under the wardrobe and was lost inside the corner of the wall and the floor. Next moment I heard the heavy groaning sound of *Sushmita* from the other room. I rushed in there. Doctor came after me. *Sushmita* had the whites of her eyes up and was groaning horrifyingly.

Doctor reached near her and placed a black object on her forehead. I went near and found that it was a black tourmaline. Within a few minutes, *Sushmita* was normal and looked towards us at complete amazement.

I asked, "Is it tourmaline?"

"Yes, it is. It has been used from ancient times by the magicians to create a strong repelling effect against the negative energies. Nowadays a true tourmaline is rare. And many of the users are not aware of the proper way of using it. And now this has saved your wife. You know sometimes something black saves you from another black."

Now Doctor got up on the bed in between *Soham* and *Sushmita* and checked the hair lock which had been used to tie the little fingers of them. It had turned deep red. Carefully Doctor untied it and instructed *Pragya* to keep it inside a black cloth.

Both *Sushmita* and *Soham* were at peace, the perfect sight I wanted to behold.

Next day we were on the laptop watching yesterday night's footage. In the footage, we could see things turning unusual when Doctor dropped the nails into the tonic water. As the black water started to come out of the nails a light foggy apparition took form and moved with the black water. It ended at the wall near the wardrobe.

Doctor said immediately, "*Dr Chatterjee* arrange a hoe and a bucket. Today we have to end the reason."

After I had arranged the hoe from the neighbouring construction site, *Dr Nachiketa* started to dig at the North-Eastern corner of our room right near the wardrobe. First, the plaster got off and then the construction materials. After digging for half an hour *Doctor* was in a full sweat. He kept the hoe and sat inside the dug ground and minutely checked the land closing his eyes. Then he murmured, "It is in here". He looked at *Pragya* and indicated her to bring his bag. *Doctor* took out short handle axe head mattock and continued exploring.

Within a few minutes, there was a different sound as if the tool had hit with something else. We all got curious. *Doctor* instructed *Pragya* to start working with him. I was shocked to see that it was the skeletal remains of somebody which was under the floor of our room right near the wardrobe. The dress indicated that it was a lady. She had her jewellery on. *Doctor* told *Pragya* to get away as there may be serious black magic involved. *Doctor* sat near the skeleton and put his hands on it. He did not speak for some minutes. When he opened his eyes he was upset. He removed the ruined clothes and there was a greater surprise waiting for us. Inside the womb of the mother, there was a small skeletal remains of an immature baby. The total scene indicated a horrible incident.

In the meantime, *Sushmita* had been there. She asked *Doctor*, "What happened *Doctor*?"

She was *Ashalata*. Around eighty years back she was murdered in this house. After a long waiting of fifteen years, she conceived and was fanatic about her coming baby. Her emotional attachment to her baby was beyond imagination. But then one day one tantric prophesied that her baby will bring death and destruction to her family and she should abort the child to escape the catastrophe. She objected and rebelled. The lunatics of this house beat her to death with her unborn child and buried her over here.

Out of strong attachment with her baby, she could not get another body and was trapped in here for long. The *Soham's* subtle touch made her free and she visualized her son in *Soham*. She loved her so much that she was not satisfied to stay inside *Soham*, rather she could not tolerate sharing *Soham* with his parents. So she decided to take *Soham* permanently in her world.

Sushmita was sobbing looking at the skeleton with the baby skeleton inside her womb.

"What to do now?" I asked in a bewildered state.

"She is now with us. Listening to us. Her sinners are already punished by her. It is time for us to do the proper rites of her and her unborn child," Doctor looked dejected.

"Shall we burn the body"? Asked *Pragya?*

"No burning will not work. We are not approved to burn her body. She must be washed away with everything here in the river and then this place must be purified through proper rituals. I shall instruct you everything properly. You need to put here one *Narmedashwara Lingam* and worship it regularly till you live in this house."

Doctor Nachiketa left us the next day with all arrangements. We did all works as he instructed. After that day there was not a bit of feeling about the existence of that spirit. *Soham* was vibrant and childish again. He remembers Doctor very well."

Dr Dey got up from his seat and mused a bit and then said, "Your story seems to be all real but until I meet *Dr Nachiketa*, there always lingers a doubt. You know often people speak highly of them whom they admire the most"

"I wish you met *Dr Nachiketa* once", *Dr.Chatterjee* beamed with pride.

Dr Sen listened with intent as if he was lost in the graphic detail of the whole experience. He grew a desire to encounter *Dr.Nachiketa.*

DARK SHADOWS ATTACK SOUMI

At the dinner table, *Dr Sen* was silent. *Soumi* was absent-minded and she was stirring her food in utmost reluctance. *Dr Sen* looked at her with irritation. *Soumi* looked as if she was unwilling in everything, unrest in the corner of her consciousness. *Soumali Sen, Soumi's* Mother noticed it and said-

"*Soumi*, finish your food quickly or it will get cold. *Dr Sen* noticed that *Soumi* hardly ate any food. But this time *Dr.Sen* did not preach his principles rather chose to be patient.

It was almost night twelve but *Dr.Sen* was working on his laptop. *Soumali* was in sleep under the blanket. She remains busy whole day. She rather lives in her world. But *Dr Sen* was happy that she was very much caring and conscious of her family. She does not allow any loophole in family issues. A happy family begins with a caring wife and mother. She is the main running force in the family.

Thoughts about *Soumali* reminded *Dr Sen* about *Sushmita*, wife of *Dr Chatterjee* and how they had handled their family issues. This inspired him about fighting the delicate odds of the family. Suddenly he planned to check about *Dr Nachiketa's* social existence. He googled *Dr Nachiketa's* name. The results did not give anything in positive. Then he searched about ghosts and spirits. At around one he got under the blanket and tried not to make the night a waste.

It was a bit colder than other usual nights. *Dr Sen* hardly had a cat nap when he was aroused with the sound of something falling in the balcony *.Dr. Sen* got up and reached the balcony. It was very cold and foggy there. The garden in front was hardly visible. While inspecting the source of the sound, *Dr Sen* discovered *Soumi* in her balcony standing at the edge of the wooden fence. It was not very clear even what she was doing there. He was utterly puzzled and angry at her behaviour. He called his wife and showed her *Soumi* at the balcony. *Soumali* looked worried. She went through the bedroom door and reached *Soumi's* room and then the balcony .*Dr.Sen* followed her. On reaching she found that *Soumi* was stretching her hands towards the garden. There was a deep layer of fog. Her face and hands were not visible as if her head and hands have entered another world.

Mrs .Sen called, "*Soumi...Soumi...*"

Soumi did not reply. *Mrs Sen* shook her by the hand and with a tremble, *Soumi* took two steps back and started crying. She had been in tears and she was almost frozen. In sudden and worrying haste, she said-

"Ma...Ma...there, look at there. They are there. All are there. They call me every night. Many are there. They cannot return. They are horrible. They whisper always. They don't let me sleep. Ma, save me."

Mrs Sen understood that there was something seriously wrong with her daughter. She embraced her daughter and brought her back in her room.

Dr Sen realized that there was a serious bone in the throat. He stood at the balcony and looked into the garden. Except for fog and cold nothing, he could behold. In the North-Eastern corner of the garden, he could spot a nebulous figure of a hut.

Dr Sen and *Mrs Sen* did not take the matter lightly. *Dr Sen* decided to know more about the house and the garden. So he went to *Mr Samanta's* house from whom *Dr Sen* had bought this house, *The Seventh Heaven*. Upon enquiry, *Mr Samanta* said that the house he got from his relative *Suryasamanta Mishra* .*Mr. Surayasamanta Mishra* and his family had disappeared mysteriously one day and till today there is no news about them. *Mr Samanta* could not give any information about the garden.

Next night *Dr Sen* did not want *Soumi* to sleep alone. He called *Sanjana*, the attendant of his clinic to sleep with her. *Sanjana* is very alert about everything, so *Dr. Sen* was at ease at night. Besides *Soumi* always enjoyed the company of *Sanjana* .*Dr. Sen* locked the door of *Soumi's* room opening into the balcony. At around night twelve *Dr Sen* bade good night to both. Today *Soumi* looked a bit vibrant and happy. But still, there was a tinge of discomfort. *Dr Sen* did not sleep until night one.

At around night three *Sanjana* shouted from *Soumi's* room .*Dr. Sen* jumped out of his bed in utmost urgency and rushed into *Soumi's* room. *Mrs Sen* also followed. Opening the door *Dr Sen* stopped abruptly for a moment. *Sanjana* was at one corner of the room horrified with her hands covering her mouth. *Soumi* was standing near the window opening into the balcony. The room was filled with fog at different places and there *Dr Sen* noticed a lot of black coloured frogs jumping all around the room in different places. And they were covered with smoky fog. Within a moment a lot of crows flew and entered the room and started flying around *Soumi. Mrs Sen* pushed *Dr Sen* and hustled towards *Soumi. Dr Sen* had his eyes protruded when he noticed that *Sanjana* was lifted a bit in the air. When *Mrs Sen* reached *Soumi,* there all could see a few pair of hands.

Through the fog came into view a few black pair of hands. *Mrs Sen* held *Soumi* and brought *Soumi* with her in the middle of the room away from those crows and hands. *Soumi* fainted immediately. Slowly the foggy frog apparitions, crows and the hands got vanished. The room seemed a bit clearer now. The face of *Soumi* looked withered and wan.

Next day *Soumi* was in high fever *.Dr. Sen* said to his wife, "Call your sister here. You three will stay together in our room. Tonight I shall stay in *Soumi's* room. Today I have to find a way to this."

Mrs Sen replied, "Yes, I am calling her, but I think we must leave this house. Something is here dangerous."

"Wait, I shall see what happens."

That day *Dr Sen* moved every corner of the garden searching something that may give him an idea of what might be the reason behind those incidents. But everything seemed to him to be normal like other gardens.

Around night nine *Dr Sen* had talks with his sister-in-law and to his wife and came into the room of *Soumi*. He slowly surveyed the room and, then opened the door of the balcony and stood there if something pops up giving him a clue. Only darkness prevailed.

In the corner of the garden, *Dr Sen* located the cottage that he had spotted earlier. He thought to start with that cottage. He wondered if the people living there have also experienced something.

Out of the house, *Dr Sen* took the gravelled path and reached near the cottage. The front yard of the cottage was filled with all flower trees. Through the flower trees, *Dr Sen* reached the veranda of the cottage. The veranda was also filled with the potted flower plants. As *Dr Sen* got up on the veranda, a voice called out, " *Babu*, come in. I knew you would come to me. Now you know what are those Invisibles."

There was a dim light glowing from inside the cottage, with the most probability of a lantern. Slowly the door opened and Dr Sen immediately recognized him. He was that strange patient who had vanished from his clinic a few days before.

In a bewildered state Dr Sen said, "You? You live in this cottage?"

"*Ha Babu*, I have been living here for forty years. Come inside *Babu*. Please sit down."

Dr Sen got inside the cottage and sat down on a plastic chair. The room is poorly but properly furnished. It looks a bit dirty from outside but the inside of the house is clean. There are two windows. One facing East and another facing the West opening to the garden. *Dr Sen* noticed two photographs. One of a lady of about forty and a boy of six or seven.

Dr Sen decided to broach the topic. He said, "I wanted to ask you …."

The man stopped *Dr Sen* in the middle and said-

"I know you want to know about this garden. About those things which disturb you at night and those who have made you afraid." Then with a pause, he resumed, “Every night from twelve to three this garden changes to something else. A land of dark shadows. They move everywhere and enchant people those who see them.”

Then all on a sudden he protruded his eyes and said-

“Everyone cannot see them. I can see them. My little *Suraj* could see them.” He pointed to the picture of the boy hanging on the wall.

Dr Sen looked at the innocent picture of the boy again. The man continued-

“My name is *Manab*. I had a happy family. My wife and son had been with me. I was like a bird always singing.” One summer night we experienced the most horrifying thunderstorm. Throughout the night it had been death fires falling around us. We thought it to be the end of us. In the morning we were alive with the thunderstorm gone. But the whole garden was burnt. We were happy that we were not hit by the thunder. But hardly did we know then that the thunder had actually given birth to some other things.

Since that day my son changed. He would only look at the garden, eat nothing and turned dispirited. One night I woke up with the sounds of some whispers and found that my son was out of the bed. I searched for him but he was not in the room. Suddenly out of the window I saw that he was there in the garden and around him, there were many shadows moving. I shouted after him. He did not listen. Slowly he moved towards deeper in the garden. I ran after him frantically but did not get him. Wildly I searched him throughout the garden but he was lost.

I did not get him back. Every night from twelve to three the garden turns the land of the dark shadows. If they see you once they will take you there. They are invincible. I tried to fight them a lot of ways but, could not do anything. Instead, whenever I go in there I see darkness and sometimes shadows moving. Many times I was wounded by those invisible forces. Still, I search for my son sitting here near the window. I hear shouts of many who are taken and trapped. I wish I were taken by them so that I could meet my son." *Manab* looked dejected.

Dr Sen asked, "Then why don't I see them and hear them?"

"I do not know. At first, I said people about this and they thought me to be mad. I do not tell anybody anymore. But I know it very well that the family who lived there before you came had seen and heard them. At first, the very little cute girl was missing and then slowly the whole family got vanished. After that, for many years no one came to live here. And now you came and I am sure you will be in trouble. That is why I came that day to warn you so that you can save you and your family."

Suddenly the clock struck twelve and *Manab* went impatient and said, "*Babu*, now they will be alive here." Saying this he looked through the window and with excitement said, "Look at there. Can you see those shadows? They are horrible."

Dr Sen looked out of the window but he did not see anything but the umbrage garden with trees.

Dr Sen was questioning himself about the rationality of the things happening around. He could only hear cold wind blowing.

Suddenly *Manab* shouted, "*Babu*, your daughter. They are taking away your daughter. She is getting lost, lost forever. I can see them hanging around her. They have held her. *Babu* saves her, save her."

With unaccustomed agility, *Dr Sen* rushed out of the cottage of *Manab*. From *Manab's* cottage to his house it is hardly a hundred meters. On the way, *Dr Sen* tumbled twice. On reaching the gate, he discovered that the door was locked from inside. He called out the names of his wife and his sister-in-law but none responded. As *Dr Sen* knew the importance of every minute he decided to take the other ways. He knew that one of the windows of his clinic room opened like a casement without any bars. He reached the window and luckily found it ajar. He jumped into the room and sprang upwards into the room and then into the balcony and then he was bewildered to see that *Soumi* was standing on the railings of the balcony.His wife and sister-in-law stood frozen staring at *Soumi. Soumi* spread her both the hands in the dense fog and *Dr Sen* understood that two black hands were holding *Soumi's* hands. He embraced *Soumi* by her waist and tried to pull down. She was held on from the other side. Now *Dr Sen* shouted, “Leave her. You can't take her. Slowly the hands released the hold off *Soumi's* hands and disappeared in the darkness. *Dr Sen* brought *Soumi* down in a senseless state. His wife and sister-in-law also came to senses. They spent the rest of the night without any sleep.

DOCTOR NACHIKETA AT DR.SEN'S HOUSE

In the very fine morning, *Dr Sen* without having any dual thought contacted *Dr Chatterjee* and acquainted him with everything and requested him to make sure the presence of *Dr Nachiketa.*

By morning eight *Dr Chatterjee* confirmed the arrival of *Dr Nachiketa*. And by two pm, *Dr Nachiketa* reached *The Seventh Heaven* by the car of *Dr Chatterjee*. *Dr Sen* had heard of *Dr Nachiktea* from *Dr Chatterjee*. Now got to meet him. Shooting out of the car *Dr. Nachiketa* beamed and shook hands with *Dr Sen* and said with a broad smile-

"It is nice to meet you, *Dr Sen*".

Dr Sen stood in amazement for *Dr Nachiketa* seemed to him to be a much-known person. With him, there was *Pragya* as he had heard from Dr *Chatterjee*. She looked like a portrait of beauty and intelligence. *Dr*

Sen had all *Dr Nachiketa's* luggage kept inside and showed their rooms. *Dr Nachiketa* said,-

"We are not here for holiday, *Dr Sen*. We would like to get to work. At first, tell me everything that has happened.

After listening to everything *Dr Nachiketa* said, "*Dr Sen*, this creation is very mysterious. The principles on which everything revolves are even very complex. Perhaps we are at the verge of one such complex issue. We have to give priority to certain things.

Firstly, we have to protect *Soumi*.

Secondly, we need to know the mystery behind this garden and thirdly, we must try to search the people who are already lost in the dark. But before that, I want to meet *Soumi*."

Dr Nachiketa came into the room where *Soumi* was kept, still in trance. *Dr Sen* touched the forehead of *Soumi*. Then he took one of her hands and checked them properly. Then closing his eyes he held *Soumi's* right leg's thumb finger and immediately *Soumi* got up with closed eyes on the bed. Everybody in the room took a step back in fear. *Dr Nachiketa* then held the left leg's little finger of *Soumi* and instructed *Pragya* to check *Soumi's* hair. *Pragya* started to check her hair but shot back in fear. From her hair started to come out a few bumblebees.

Dr Nachiketa looked at *Dr Sen* for a moment and then looking at *Pragya* said that "*Pragya* set the cameras everywhere."

In the meantime, *Manab* was called. *Dr Nachiketa* looked at him-

"Do not worry you will meet your son. That day your son did not reply to your call. This pains you a lot. But you must realise that he was in their capture. So it was not possible for him to listen to you. Next time you enter there, you must be naked; you must put your urine all over your body. Ghosts are allergic to nitrogen and your urine has nitrogen which will keep them away. And while searching your son, carry an earthen pot with burning charcoal and burn dry red chilli there with your hairs. The smoke will lead you to your son."

Dr Nachiketa instructed *Dr Chatterjee* some works and helped *Pragya* to set cameras at every corner. Since *Dr Nachiketa* came, he was on dark coffee. Many cups he had already drunk.

In the afternoon, when *Dr Nachikta* was sitting in the balcony and was sipping coffee with all others, *Somali Sen* asked-

"*Doctor*, we did not believe in spirits. But things are somewhat shaking our beliefs. What do you think, what has happened to *Soumi*? Will she be all right?"

"*Mrs Sen*, to speak very clearly, your garden is actually a portal. It is a gateway for the entities of the other dimension to access this world. It works around a certain area. I think it is not a very big area but it at least covers your garden and a bit of your house too. It does not remain active for all the time. As I have heard the incidents, it seems to me that this portal becomes active at around twelve night and continues for a few hours. Whoever gets effected by this portal, will visualize a different world which rarely, matches with ours. It cannot be exactly told which world or dimensions it is but in most of the cases the experience is nasty."

"*Babu* they would not leave anybody. Whoever sees them, they take away in their world. My son also had seen them and they took him", *Manab* reflected agony standing in one corner.

Dr Nachiketa smiled absent-mindedly and said, "I shall see them today"

"*Babu* everybody cannot see them. *Doctor Babu* cannot see. I can see. But I do not know why haven't they taken me?"

"*Manab*, my whole business is with them. What you cannot see in open eyes I can see them. I do not allow the mystery to remain a mystery. When you transcend your consciousness you can perceive what normally is not possible. Come with me. I shall show you something that I have already seen. Come to *Soumi's* room."

Everybody followed *Dr Nachiketa* in *Soumi's* room. *Soumi* was on her bed in an unconscious state. Her face was withered and a wan look made everybody dismayed.

Dr Nachiketa said to *Pragya*, "Pragya take out the infrared camera and take some pictures of the room in the darkness."

Pragya switched the lights off and took a good number of pictures with Kodak infrared camera film. *Doctor* took those films and using his projector reflected on the opposite wall. *Doctor* changed the colours of the images and slowly everybody could see images of the footsteps on the wall, on the floor and everywhere of the room.

Dr Nachiketa now took out a stick with a light at the end of it and took it near the face of *Soumi* and there had been black spots near her neck, cheeks and hands. *Dr Nachiketa* said-

"Whenever you feel much cold you must realise that negative energies are stronger around you and the portal is very intensely active."

Mrs Sen started crying. She said, "Doctor, please save my daughter. We are almost dead seeing her in this situation."

"Do not worry *Mrs Sen*, everything will be all right."

Dr.Sen spoke in an undertone, "I think, we must leave this house and this is going to be the only way to get rid of this trouble."

"No *Dr Sen*, we are not with this option anymore. Look at your daughter. She is already there in that world. You have her body here with her basic system running, but it is temporary. Tonight if they get access of *Soumi* again your daughter will simply disappear from here. Our first priority is to bring *Soumi* back from there. But at the same time, we must remember that during high negative energy there is a great possibility of one our getting trapped in there. So we must have our protection at first."

Dr Nachiketa now looked at *Pragya* and said, "*Pragya*, take the white Agate stones out."

Pragya opened one of the bags brought by *Dr Nachiketa* and took out a black cloth. From there she took out some white coloured stones .*Dr. Nachiketa* gave everybody one Agate stone and said, "This is very rare Agate stones. This has the properties of repelling negative energies of the highest level. In case the energy level is too high it will simply turn grey or black in colour. Remember, you have to keep it in your hand. It must stay in touch with your body."

"And what about *Soumi*? She is already trapped. Won't you do anything so that she is protected?" Mrs Sen was worried.

"Yes, I have already instructed *Dr Chatterjee* to bring a special kind of a chair for *Soumi*. The chair is precisely made for this purpose. I have a contact in here who has consented to give the same. The chair creates a strong certain magnetic field which will not allow those entities to reach them and in this way we shall never lose the physical self of *Soumi*."

"This is all about protection. But how will she be fine again?" *Mrs Sen* uttered the words sobbing.

"Yes, tonight I shall go into that world and bring *Soumi* back. And I have arranged for you all an opportunity to experience the whole world. This experience is not going to be a physical one rather a psychic one. I shall guide you down to the frequency to experience the whole event."

Saying this *Dr Nachiketa* took out a small device with a bulb at the top of it. Then he took out some headphone type devices.

"This is a device created by me. This is a combination of light and sound. This bulb will go on blinking in accordance to the sound. The sound will create a binaural beat of around 4hz. And then I shall guide you to there. But there must be one person attending here. If anyone is showing signs of uneasiness of choking of breath, he/she must take the headphone out and take the person away.

Manab Said, “I shall be there to see that everyone is fine”.

“Then get ready we shall start everything probably at twelve night,” and *Dr Nachiketa* walked slowly out in the balcony gazing at the mysterious garden.

DOCTOR SAVES SOUMI FROM THE SHADOWS

Night eleven fifty everybody gathered in *Soumi's* room. In the middle of the room on a table, there is a table on which there was a machine kept. Around the table in the right-hand side, there are *Mr Sen and Mrs Sen*. On the left-hand side, Dr.Chatterjee and Pragya are sitting. All are with their headphones on. On the South facing the north and the balcony extending to the garden, Dr Nachiketa was sitting and opposite to him on the specially made chair, there was unconscious *Soumi.*

Outside the room slowly the fog started to become dense and has already reached the balcony. A little while before, the garden was all noisy with the sounds of the cricket, cicada and beetle. Now the whole garden has gone silent. Slowly everybody noticed that from under the door thick fog is spreading into the room and made the room and the floor foggy.

Dr Nachiketa said-

"Now we shall begin it. Remember, you have to be with the headphone and follow my instructions properly. You are protected by the *Agate* stone. So do not worry about safety. Do not talk with any entities. There may be illusions created. Do not react."

Now *Dr Nachiketa* switched the device on and the bulb on the top of the device started to blink at a certain pace and *Dr.Nachiketa* said-

"Listen to the sound and follow my instructions carefully."

Slowly the sound started to get slow and blinking of the light got slower.

Dr.Nachiketa said-

"Follow my voice. Let the darkness in. Come down deeper and deeper until you see me. I am down there in the darkness waiting for you. Slowly all transcended the present state and reached the realm of the subconscious. First, they were in somewhere in the darkness. Slowly all could see *Dr.Nachiketa* standing with an amiable face.

It was even foggy over there; the place looked like a barren land. The place was dark but still things were visible. *Dr.Nachiketa* waved his hand to follow him. *Doctor* started to walk and passed a few bushy plants. After a while, all could see a place where a fire was burning. Some fellows were sitting around the fire. *Doctor* passed near them but they did not even care to look at him. Now *Doctor* started to walk through a narrow lane with walls on both sides. The end of the wall could not be seen for darkness. After *Doctor* moved a bit further, he could see the lane blocked by some dark shadows. As he got nearer the shadows started to grow in number. They had glowing eyes. All could see dark faces with glowing eyes. Slowly something started to glow in the hand of *Dr.Nachiketa*.It dispersed the dark shadows. The lane was clean now. *Doctor* moved forward.

After he crossed the lane, all could see a black pond. And through the fog all could see *Soumi*, sitting and crying. She was not out of her senses, rather she was looking at the shadows around her. She was sitting in the middle of the pond. It was not clear whether there was a platform on the water, but she could be seen on the chair. The chair was actually that special chair where *Soumi* was made to sit on.

Dr.Nachiketa reached near the pond. Surprising everybody he got down into the pond. Walking slowly in the pond, he was moving towards *Soumi.* There started a sudden movement in the shadows which were around *Soumi.* The shadows turned unrest and moved fast towards *Dr.Nachiketa.*But before it could reach *Dr Nachiketa*, Doctor took out a crystal which started emanating light. The shadows were deflected by the crystal light. *Dr, Nachiketa* slowly started to move towards *Soumi.* When he was a little away from *Soumi*, all the shadows started to move around *Soumi* and enter her body. *Soumi* started bleeding through her nose.

Here inside the room, *Manab* could see *Soumi* bleeding through her nose and could not decide what to do. He went crazy. He rushed to and fro in the room. With suppressed anguish, *Manab* said, "I cannot see you gone. You will not be gone like my son. I shall save you at any cost."

Then *Manab* paused and had a sudden flush of determination on his face and then decided something.

Dr.Nachiketa reached near *Soumi* and placed the crystal on her head. Slowly all the shadows started to move out of the body of *Soumi*. Within minutes *Soumi* disappeared from the chair and *Dr.Nachiketa* collapsed in the chair. The crystal fell off his hand in the water of the pond. All the shadows gathered over *Dr.Nachiketa*.He could hardly be seen. *The doctor* was holding his neck as if he was being choked. Then a hand was seen shot out of the pond water. The hand pulled *Doctor* inside the pond. But who pulled the doctor in the pond was not clear. It was the hand of a human and not of shadows. His face could not be seen.

Back in the room all came to their senses. *Dr Nachiketa* was all wet with water. He was smiling sitting in the chair. He said-

"Soumi is safe now. She is out of the clutches of the shadows. Both *Mrs Sen* and *Dr Sen* embraced *Soumi* who was all a changed girl now.

"Thanks a lot, *Doctor*. I heard of you and today I saw you and I know that you are a saviour truly," *Dr Sen* was ecstatic.

"This creation is very mysterious and complex. As fishes do not understand water even if they live in the water, similarly we are a part of the creation without being aware of the creation. Everything is inside us. All we need to do is to understand who we are and the mist of the ignorance will be cleared."

Then *Dr Nachiketa* got up from his chair and said-

"Now let us get out of this house immediately. It is not safe anymore."

After half an hour all got out of the house. But nobody noticed that *Manab* was not there anywhere. Where is *Manab*?

OTHER BOOKS BY THE AUTHOR

1. KALCHAKRA -OOM AND THE CHOSEN FIVE

2. 1001 ONE WORD SUBSTITUTIONS FOR COMPETITIVE EXAMINATIONS.

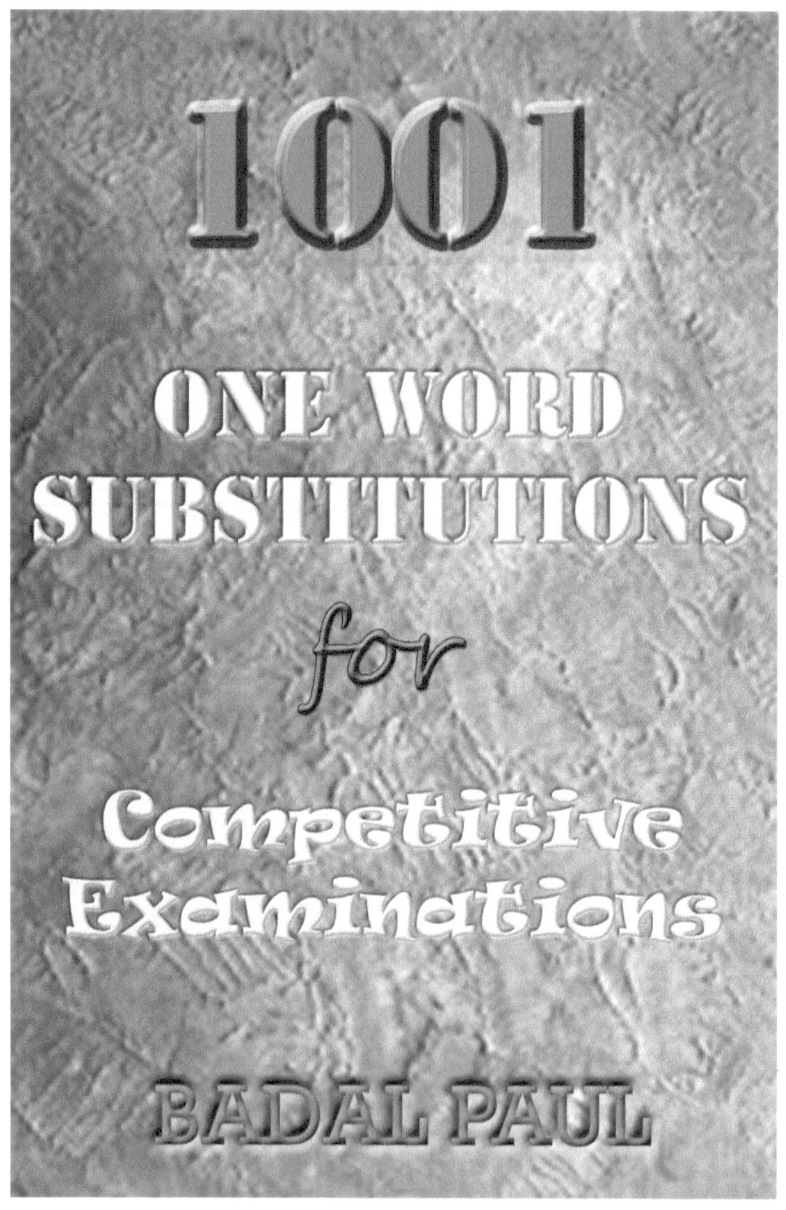

STAY CONNECTED FOR THE SECOND PART OF THE HORROR SERIES -

"WHISPERS OF THE INVISIBLES

RETURN OF RUDRA"

www.ingramcontent.com/pod-product-compliance
Lightning Source LLC
LaVergne TN
LVHW101926220826
846093LV00009B/380
* 9 7 8 9 3 5 2 6 8 2 5 3 9 *